BRIGHT and EARLY BOOKS for BEGINNING Beginners

Ants are amazing.

That's why
angry ants advanced
across an apple,
an acorn,
an apricot,
an ax,
an angleworm,
an alligator,
Aunt Alice's airplane,
Avenue A,
apes' apartments,
and all Arizona!

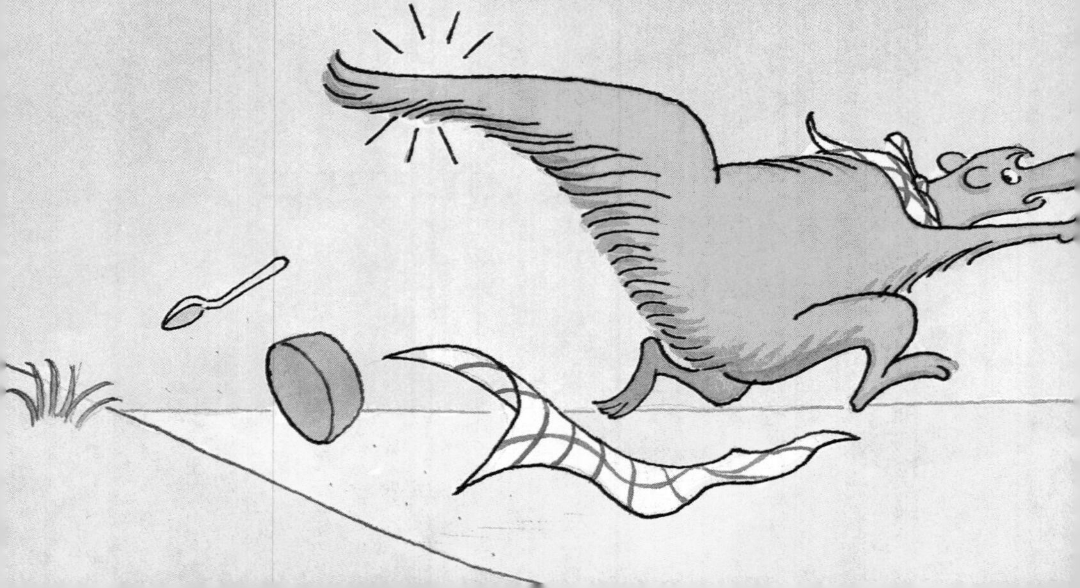

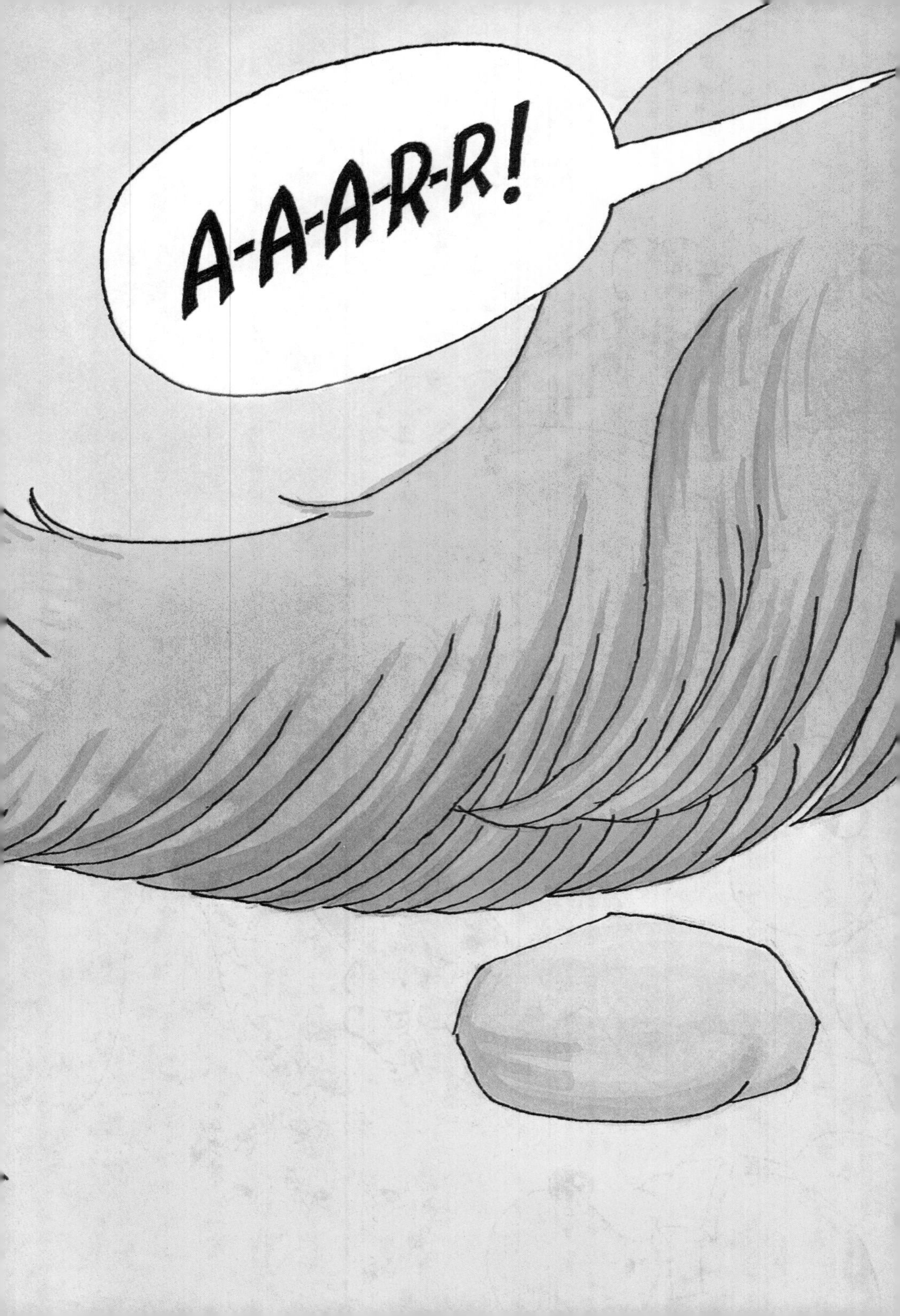
A-A-A-R-R!

ATTACK!

Aha!
An anteater
and
an anthill!

Why do angry ants
advance across
an apple,
an acorn,
an apricot,
an ax,
an angleworm,
an alligator,
Aunt Alice's airplane,
Avenue A,
apes' apartments,
and all Arizona?

ARIZO

ARIZONA

—and <u>all</u> <u>Arizona</u>!

Angry ants
advance across
apes' apartments

and across Avenue A.

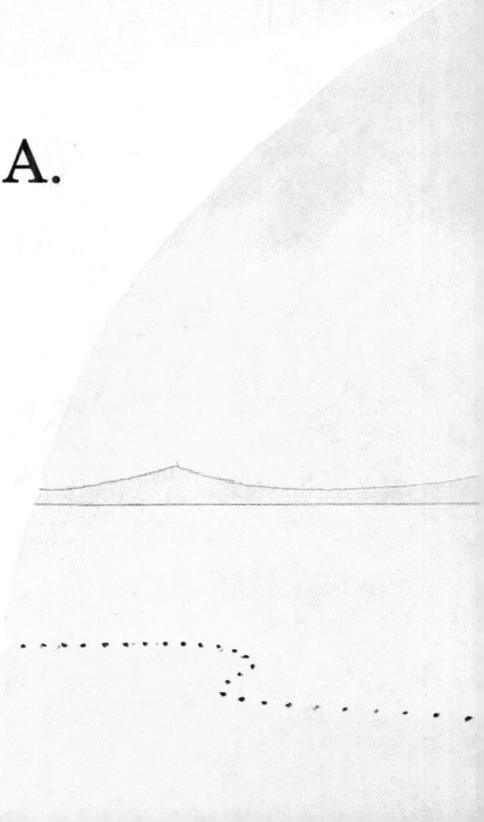

and Aunt Alice's airplane,

Angry ants
advance across
an alligator

Why do angry ants
advance across
an apple,
an acorn,
an apricot,
an ax,
and an angleworm?

across an apricot,

an ax,

and an angleworm.

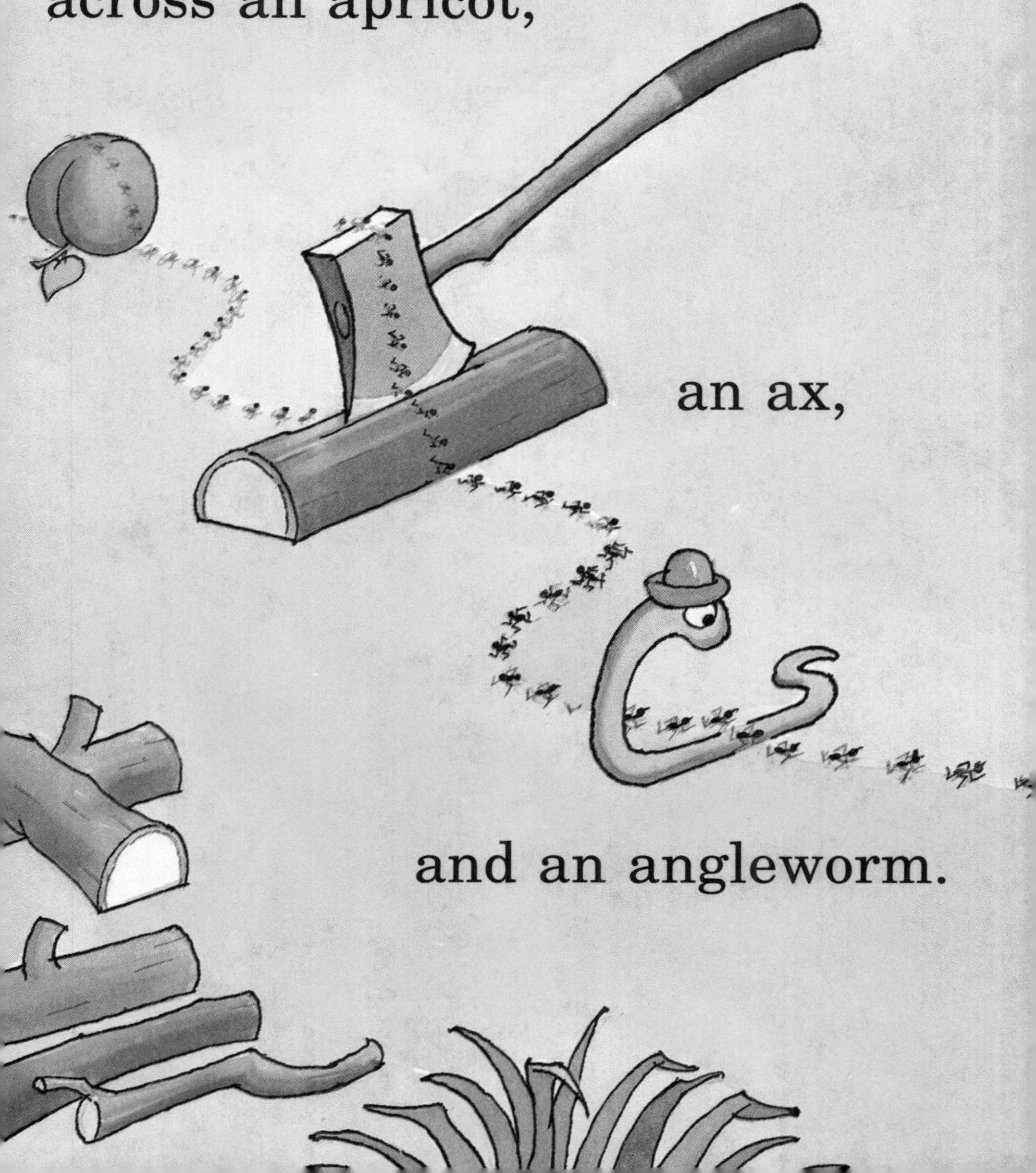

Angry ants
advance across
an apple
and an acorn,

across an acorn.

—across an apple,

Angry ants advance

Ants

Ant

Stan & Jan Berenstain

A Bright and Early Book
From BEGINNER BOOKS
A Division of Random House, Inc.

Published in the United States by Random House, Inc., New York,
and simultaneously in Canada by Random House of Canada Limited, Toronto.

http://www.randomhouse.com/

Library of Congress Cataloging-in-Publication Data
Berenstain, Stan, 1923–
The Berenstains' A book / [Stan & Jan Berenstain].
p. cm. — (A bright and early book)
SUMMARY: An army of angry ants march across and around
all sorts of items that begin with the letter "a."
ISBN 0-679-88705-9 (trade). — ISBN 0-679-98705-3 (lib. bdg.)
[1. Ants—Fiction. 2. Alphabet.]
I. Berenstain, Jan, 1923– II. Title. III. Series: Bright and early book.
PZ7.B4483Bfwl 1997 [E]—dc21 97-6783

Printed in the United States of America 10 9 8 7 6 5 4 3 2 1

BERENSTAINS'
A
BOOK

This book belongs to ...

____

GROLIER
BOOK CLUB EDITION

BRIGHT and EARLY BOOKS for BEGINNING Beginners